Disney's
TOONTOWN

THE TOONTOWN PLAYERS
PRESENT
Chicken
Little

Written by Margaret Snyder

Illustrated by Darrell Baker and Robbin Cuddy

MERRIGOLD PRESS • NEW YORK

The play was about to start. Mickey gave Goofy the signal to raise the curtain. Goofy hurried across the stage to pull the curtain rope, but instead he caught his foot in it. *Crash!*

"A-hyuck!" Goofy laughed, then cleared his throat. "Ah, well. The show must go on. Ladies and gentlemen, the Toontown Players proudly present *Chicken Little,* starring Daisy Duck as . . . uh . . . as . . . uh . . . as Chicken Little!"

One day, while Chicken Little was standing under a tree, something fell and hit her on the head with a **KERPLUNK**.

"What was that?" Chicken Little wondered, looking around. Seeing nothing, she assumed that something terrible was happening. "The sky must be falling!" Chicken Little peeped. "I have to warn Goosey Loosey."

So Chicken Little ran along and ran along until she found Goosey Loosey. "The sky is falling! The sky is falling!" Chicken Little cried.

"Oh, my!" said Goosey Loosey. "How do you know?"

"Because something hit me on the head with a *kerplunk*!" said Chicken Little.

"Not a KERPLUNK?" said Goosey Loosey, her eyes open wide.

"Yes, a KERPLUNK," Chicken Little replied.

"Owie!" cried Goosey Loosey. "The sky must be falling! Let's go warn Ducky Lucky."

So Chicken Little and Goosey Loosey ran along and ran along until they found Ducky Lucky. "The sky is falling! The sky is falling!" the two birds shouted.

"Scout's honor?" asked Ducky Lucky.

"Scout's honor!" said Chicken Little.

"How do you know?" asked Ducky Lucky.

"Because something hit me on the head with a *kerplunk*!" said Chicken Little.

"Not the dreaded KERPLUNK?" said Ducky Lucky.

"Yes, the dreaded KERPLUNK," said Chicken Little.

"Ooh! That smarts!" cried Ducky Lucky. "The sky *must* be falling! Let's go warn Turkey Lurkey."

So Chicken Little, Goosey Loosey, and Ducky Lucky ran along and ran along until they found Turkey Lurkey. "The sky is falling! The sky is falling!" the three birds shouted.

"You're pulling my leg!" said Turkey Lurkey.

"No, really, Turkey Lurkey, I was hit on the head with a **KERPLUNK**!" said Chicken Little.

"A real **KERPLUNK**?" asked Turkey Lurkey.

"A real **KERPLUNK**," said Chicken Little.

"Well, you can't ignore a *kerplunk*!" cried Turkey Lurkey. "The sky *must* be falling! Let's go warn the King."

So Chicken Little, Goosey Loosey, Ducky Lucky, and Turkey Lurkey ran along and ran along on their way to find the King. But then they met Foxy Loxy lounging in the grass beneath a shady tree. "Just where are you birds headed?" asked Foxy Loxy.

The birds looked at each other nervously. They had heard many stories about Foxy Loxy's trickery. "Well," said Chicken Little bravely, "the sky is falling, and we're going to warn the King."

"The *sky* is falling!" snickered Foxy Loxy. "Why do you think the sky is falling?"

"Because something fell and hit me on the head with a KERPLUNK," said Chicken Little.

Foxy Loxy laughed loudly. He knew that birds could be silly, but this was ridiculous. "Hit you with a **KERPLUNK**?" he sneered. "You birdbrain. There's no way the sky is falling!"

Just then an enormous acorn fell out of the tree and hit Foxy Loxy on the head with a **KERPLUNK**! Foxy Loxy jumped and looked around but didn't *see* anything.

"The sky *is* falling! The sky *is* falling!" Foxy Loxy shouted, racing off through the meadow.

Chicken Little, Goosey Loosey, Ducky Lucky, and Turkey Lurkey watched Foxy Loxy running in circles until they heard chattering coming from a tree. They looked up to see two squirrels playing in the branches.

"Oops, sorry!" the squirrels called down to the birds. "That's the second acorn we've dropped today!"

"That was the second?" said Chicken Little. "Where did you drop the first acorn?"

"Over near the barn," the first squirrel answered.

"Yeah!" said the other squirrel. "It **KERPLUNKED** a little chicken! A little chicken who looks just like you, as a matter of fact."

"Aha!" said Chicken Little, Goosey Loosey, Ducky Lucky, and Turkey Lurkey. "Then the sky *isn't* falling."

"We haven't noticed anything," said the squirrels, "and being up in the trees, we'd be the first to know."

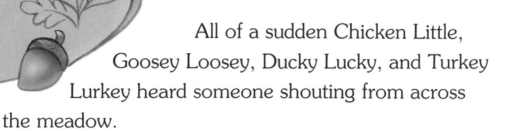

All of a sudden Chicken Little, Goosey Loosey, Ducky Lucky, and Turkey Lurkey heard someone shouting from across the meadow.

"The sky is falling! The sky is falling!" the voice called out. It was Foxy Loxy warning his fox friends.

"Do you think we should tell him the sky isn't falling?" asked Goosey Loosey.

The bird friends all looked at each other. "Naah," they said in unison.

So Chicken Little, Goosey Loosey, Ducky Lucky, and Turkey Lurkey went along and went along until they reached home. And after that day, whenever something fell and hit Chicken Little on the head with a KERPLUNK, she always checked the trees for squirrels.

As the play ended, the Toontown Players came to the edge of the stage and took their bows. Goofy was about to lower the curtain, when THUNK! He pulled the wrong rope. Goofy picked himself up and looked around.

"Gawrsh!" said Goofy. "Maybe the sky *is* falling! A-hyuck."